Michael D. Stansbie lives with his wife, Mary, in a small town in central coastal Queensland, Australia. He is a presenter on the radio and has written short stories and radio plays.

Through experiences travelling extensively all over the world, his creativity has been inspired by these travels.

This book of short stories is his first to be published.

To Mary, Jaffa, and Paul Macfarlane, A.K.A. The Rat.

Michael D. Stansbie

A Book of Stories

Austin Macauley Publishers™
LONDON · CAMBRIDGE · NEW YORK · SHARJAH

Copyright © Michael D. Stansbie 2024

The right of Michael D. Stansbie to be identified as author of this work has been asserted by the author in accordance with sections 77 and 78 of the Copyright, Designs and Patents Act 1988.

All rights reserved. No part of this publication may be reproduced, stored in a retrieval system, or transmitted in any form or by any means, electronic, mechanical, photocopying, recording, or otherwise, without the prior permission of the publishers.

Any person who commits any unauthorised act in relation to this publication may be liable to criminal prosecution and civil claims for damages.

This is a work of fiction. Names, characters, businesses, places, events, locales, and incidents are either the products of the author's imagination or used in a fictitious manner. Any resemblance to actual persons, living or dead, or actual events is purely coincidental.

A CIP catalogue record for this title is available from the British Library.

ISBN 9781035868612 (Paperback)
ISBN 9781035868629 (ePub e-book)

www.austinmacauley.com

First Published 2024
Austin Macauley Publishers Ltd®
1 Canada Square
Canary Wharf
London
E14 5AA

The crew at Austin Macauley Publishers. Without them, none of this would have happened. Mary, who kept pushing me when I wanted to stop. Bob Leatham. Brian Roberts and Evergreen for their computer skills. Last but not least, my family.

Table of Contents

Wombat Springs Race Day	**11**
Halley's Treasure	**23**
Harold The Bandit	**33**
The Voyage of The Empire Rose	**41**
The Travels of Squirrel Little Bottom	**50**
Retribution	**60**

Wombat Springs Race Day

Queensland, Australia
February 1952

The bus makes its way slowly up the slight rise and stops in a cloud of dust outside the Wombat Springs Hotel. The driver opens the door, and a young woman alights. She is tall with a good figure and dark, glossy shoulder-length hair. She is wearing a white blouse with a knee-length dark skirt and ankle boots. While she waits for the driver to get her case, she studies her surroundings. The hotel is a single-storey weatherboard building with a raised, wide, roofed verandah at the front and down one side. Along the verandah are tables and chairs. Some outbuildings can be seen over the fence that go from each side of the hotel. She gazes along the road and can see some buildings that mark the edge of the small town. Across from the hotel, all that is to be seen, as far as the horizon, is dry grass with the odd shrub and stunted tree.

The front doors of the hotel open, and a woman walks out and down the steps. She is probably in her late fifties with faded blonde hair and a stout figure. She is wearing a dress covered by an apron and walks towards the young woman.

She extends her hand. 'You must be Katrina, our new barmaid. Welcome to Wombat Springs.'

The woman takes the proffered hand. 'That's right, call me Kat, and you must be Mrs Dongle.' 'Please call me Sheila.' Just then, a young man comes through the doors with a trolley. He approaches them. Sheila does the introductions. 'Kat, this is young Jack, he's our odd job man. Jack, this is Kat, our new barmaid.' Jack blushes and removes his cap. 'Pleased to meet you, miss. I'll just get the supplies, Missus.' He takes the trolley to the back of the bus. The driver approaches them and hands Kat a suitcase. 'There you go, miss. G'day, Sheila, how's it goin'?' 'Good thanks, Joe.' 'Right. I'll go and unload your supplies.' Sheila takes the case. 'Come on, Kat, let's get you settled in.' They enter the hotel. The main room is perhaps twenty yards long and half as wide. Down the right-hand side is the bar and on the left are tables and chairs. Sheila says, 'This is the public bar. On the left, through those glass doors is the Ladies lounge and dining room with its own bar. As you can see, we have a small stage at the end. We get singers or bands when we can. To the left is the Ladies loo and the Gents is on the right.' They go through a short passageway, past the Ladies Toilets. 'This is our staff accommodation. You can use me and my husband's toilet and bathroom. Here's your key. I'll leave you to settle in. I'll be serving afternoon tea at three o'clock in the dining room. See ya then.'

After leaving the hotel, the bus enters the town and pulls up in front of the General Store and Post Office. The driver opens the door, and a young woman alights. She is medium height, slim, with short blonde hair. She is dressed in tan slacks and matching jacket. The driver deposits two suitcases by the door of the general store. The door opens, and a tall man in his fifties comes out and looks at the girl. 'G'day. I'm Stan Fairweather. You must be the new school teacher.' 'That's right, Beatrice Browning. How do you do?' 'Very well, thank you. You'll be staying at Miss Fogerty's boarding house. I'll get our Dave to take your things and show you the way.' 'I would be most grateful. Thank you.'

Stan leans in through the door of the shop and calls out, 'Dave, bring out the trolley and take the new school teacher and her things to Miss Fogerty's house.' Dave turns out to be a boy of about twelve. He loads the suitcase onto the trolley and says to Beatrice, 'If you would like to follow me, miss, it's not far.' As they set off, she turns to him. 'Do you go to the school, Dave?' 'Yes, miss, I'll be in grade six this year and next year, I'll be going away to boarding school. Well, here we are.' They are in front of a two-storey brick house. Dave opens the gate, and they go down a short path to a stained glass front door. Dave rings the bell. The door opens to reveal a woman in her sixties. She is short with a full figure, bright red hair, a weathered face, and a big grin. She is wearing a multicoloured dress and silver shoes. 'Hello, deary. I'm Miss Fogerty, but you can call me Madge. You must be the new teacher. The Department told me to expect you. All the teachers have stayed here. I'll get Fred, my odd job man, to take your things up to your room.' Beatrice turns to Dave. 'Here's a penny for your help.' 'Gosh, ta very much, Miss. See ya.' It's late afternoon, and Beatrice has moved into her room, freshened up, and is having a cup of tea with Madge in the dining room. Madge smiles at Beatrice. 'So, tell me about yourself, Beatrice?' 'I trained and then worked in a couple of city schools, but I'm from the country.' A small town called

Wheelabarraback. My parents own the Post Office there. I wanted to get back to the country to a small school, and here I am.' 'How long have you been here, Madge?' 'Over thirty years, buried two husbands. My son went off and joined the Navy, and I haven't seen him for years. This boarding house keeps me busy. I get the odd traveller and Government workers, and, of course, teachers.' 'I heard that the last teacher left in rather a hurry.' 'Yes, that's true. A week before the end of the year. E' was a strange one, a right toff. E had all these strange records that E used to play, opera and that. I found out later that the reason that he came out here was that the Department did a deal with him that if he did two years in a remote school, they would offer him a Principle's job in a city school. He didn't get on very well here at all. He thought that we were all Hillbillies. It was Sunday before the start of the last week. He came down for breakfast and demanded Caviar and lobster thermadore. I had no idea what he was on about. So he storms out of the house. We found out later that he got a flagon of moonshine off Speed Cooper. Anyway, I didn't hear him that night, and he didn't come down for breakfast, and then when he didn't turn up at the school, I went and got the constable and we went into his room and there he was, hiding under his bed and he wouldn't come out. The constable and Fred finally got him out, and they took him down to the nurse's station. His sister came out the next day and took him back to the city. I reckon that you'll do better than that.' 'I certainly hope so. Tomorrow, I'll go down to the school and get it ready for Monday.'

That same afternoon, Kat and Sheila are having afternoon tea in the pub's dining room. Kat asks, 'Have you always been in pubs, Sheila?' 'Pretty much. I was working as a barmaid at the pub that Bob was managing. We fell in love, got married, and leased a rural pub. After a few years, we borrowed enough to buy this place. It was pretty run down, but over the years we've built it up. We have been here over twenty years now. Bob really enjoys it out here. He's got his fishing and shooting. That's where he is now, out west with a couple of his mates. They should be back this afternoon.' 'Do you have any kids, Sheila?' 'Yeah, a boy and girl. Anne is in the city trying to make it as a singer, and Tony's at Uni, doing a science degree.

They came home for Christmas, but after three days, they were keen to get back to the city. It was good to see them. Normally the only time we hear from them is when they want money, but they're good kids.' 'It must be a bit lonely sometimes. Is there much to do here?' 'Luckily, the pub keeps me pretty busy, and there are the pictures once a month. And probably our busiest time is coming up in just over a month, when we sponsor the annual Wombat Springs race meeting. Kat, I think that you and I are going to get on fine. Tomorrow night, being Friday, is our busiest night, so tonight relax and have a couple of drinks. Bar meals are from six to eight. We have breakfast here at eight and then start work. Right, oh. I'll go and start setting up the bar. See ya later.'

Beatrice walks down to the school, which is on the edge of town. She opens the gate, looks around, and sees that someone has been looking after the grounds. She unlocks the door and enters. It's a timber building with one big room. Along both sides are louvre windows; she opens them to let in some breeze. There is a large pot-belly stove in the centre of the room. At one end is a large desk and several large cupboards. She counts thirty desks scattered around the room. She rolls up her sleeves and starts to organise things.

It is Monday morning at the little school, the first day of the new year. Kids are arriving by car and some on horseback. The horses are let into the paddock at the back of the school. At five minutes to nine, Beatrice stands by the door and rings a hand bell. 'Alright, children, come on in single file, please. Now you will see that the room is divided into six rows of desks. This row here is for the new kids in grade one, and the last row is for the bigger kids in grade six. If you all take a seat, I will call the roll and get to know you all. I will write my name on the blackboard. There it is, Miss Goodfellow. David, would you like to be blackboard monitor? 'Oh, yes, Miss, I did it last year.' It's the end of the day, and the kids have all gone when a buggy pulled by a lovely white horse pulls into the yard. A man alights and walks towards Beatrice. He is in his late fifties, wearing moleskin pants, a white shirt, jacket, and an Akruba hat. Beatrice greets him. 'Good afternoon.' 'And a good afternoon to you, Miss. I must say that you seem to be a vast improvement on the last teacher. My name is Ronald Weatherby. I have a sheep and wheat farm a couple of miles down the road. As I have no children of my own, if something is needed by the school, I try to help out. At the end of term, I bring some treats for the kids.' 'That's very kind of you.' She extends her hand. 'I'm Beatrice Goodfellow, pleased to meet you. I must say, that's a splendid buggy and a fine horse. I enjoy riding; I have a quarter horse back home.' 'After my wife died, I needed something to occupy myself, apart from the farm, so I built some stables and started training horses. I was mildly successful. I still train a couple for friends. Would you like to come for lunch on

Saturday? We could go for a ride after; I have a couple of horses that need a run. I take it that you're staying at Miss Fogerty's.' 'That would be very nice, Mr Weatherby.' 'Please call me Ronald. I will pick you up from the boarding house at nine thirty, if that is alright?' 'That would be lovely.'

It's Friday mid-morning at the Hotel, and Kat is setting the bar up for the night. A man walks in carrying a cardboard box. He is tall with slicked-back dark hair and a moustache, wearing a white shirt partly open, showing a gold chain. He is obviously going for the Errol Flynn look. He approaches Kat and puts the box on the bar. 'Well, hello, you must be the new girl, Kat.'

'I don't know about new, but yes, I'm Kat.' He grins, 'I'm Mickey Finn, proprietor of Midnight Auto's, the only car yard in town. I'm in the centre of town, on the hill, so I can see you coming. I've just got a new sports car in. How about coming for a spin tomorrow? I could show you the sights.' She looks him up and down and shakes her head. 'Nothing personal, but I'd rather get my tits caught in a mangle.' 'Now don't be like that.' Sheila enters. 'Like what?' Mickey turns to face her. 'G'day, Sheila, I just brought the meat trays for the raffles tonight.' 'Where did you get it?' she asks suspiciously. 'Fair go, Sheila, a cocky owed me a favour, and I am donating them' 'Okay, Mickey, thanks. Kat, can you take them out to the cool room?'

It's Friday night a week later, and the bar is packed. Sheila and Bob are behind the bar, Kat is picking up glasses and serving. She is wearing a short skirt and a low-cut top. Bob turns to Sheila. 'The locals must have heard about our Kat. I reckon every young bloke for miles is here, and some not so young,' as he eyes Mickey trying to chat with Kat. 'I think they are all out of luck,' Sheila says. 'I've noticed that our young senior constable has taken to calling in just before closing time.' 'Next week we had better start getting ready for the big race day. It's only a month away.'

Earlier that same Friday, Madge and Beatrice are in Madge's parlour. 'Well, Beatrice, how did your first week go?' 'Better than I expected. I gather that the last teacher was a bit of an ogre.' 'You know, I don't have any boarders over the weekend, so I might have a little tipple. Will you join me?' 'Sure, why not, what do you have?' 'Beer or brandy. I've got some lemonade if you would like a shandy.' 'A shandy would be just the thing.' Madge gets glasses and two bottles and makes a shandy and a brandy and lime. Beatrice raises her glass. 'Cheers.' 'I met Mr Weatherby today; he came to the school.' Madge says, 'Ah yes. Ronald, a very nice man, a real gent. So sad, his wife died in childbirth and the baby died a day later. Oh, it must be twenty years ago now. He was a lost soul until he started with the horses. It's because of him that we have our biggest day, the Wombat Springs Cup race day. It's in a month's time. Would you like another?' 'That would be lovely, but I must, as the men say, have my shout.' 'That's alright. When Fred goes to the pub to get mine, he can get whatever you want.' It's the next morning, and Roland arrives in his car. After a fifteen-minute drive, they turn down a tree-lined drive. At the end of the drive is a single-storey brick house with a verandah all around and a large chimney on one end. They drive around to the back of the house and pull up at a large barn. As they get out, a stable hand approaches. 'I'll need the two about two o'clock, thanks, Bill.' 'After Ronald has shown Beatrice around, they are in the house dining room enjoying a sherry.' Beatrice raises her glass. 'You certainly have a very nice set up, what with the stables and the track. So what is the story with the cup, Ronald?' 'After the grim days of the depression and then the war, I thought that it would be a jolly good idea to have a race meeting, where people could get together and show off their riding skills and their horses and have a jolly good time. So I had the cup made in the city and made it the prize for the main event. We had the first one in '46. I never dreamt that it would become so big.' 'So who holds the cup now?' 'Ah, that's a bit of a sore point at the moment. For the last three years, it has been won by someone from Cooper's Gully, a town thirty miles away, and the last two by a character called Squizzy Taylor. Ah, here's cook with lunch.' After lunch, they go to the stables, where two horses are saddled. Ronald mounts the chestnut and invites Beatrice to mount the Palomino.

They head out. An hour later, they return at a gallop, dismount, and hand the reins to the stable hand. Beatrice says to Ronald, 'My word, that was wonderful, thank you.' 'Anytime, and I must say that you ride very well. Let's go back to the house and have tea.' 'What!' There is a roaring sound, and a motor car fly's around the corner of the house and slides to a stop in a cloud of dust. The engine is switched off, and two men get out. One is medium build with ginger hair and a goatee. He is wearing a brown checked suit and a bow tie. He walks towards Ronald. 'What ho, Ronnie, old boy. We had to deliver a car over this way, and I says to Charlie, let's call in on my old mate Ronnie and see if he's got a nag to run in the cup. You know my jockey, Charlie.' 'Ah, yes, Charlie Saddlesore,' the man with him replies angrily. 'Saddlehorn! It's Saddlehorn,' the other man interrupts him. 'And who might this charming young lady be?' Ronald replies, 'This is Miss Goodfellow, the new school teacher. Miss Goodfellow, this is Mr Squizzy Taylor, and as you heard, his jockey, Charlie Saddlesore.' 'Saddlehorn!' Beatrice nods to the two men. 'Glad to meet you two gentlemen. Mr Weatherby has kindly offered to give me some riding lessons.' Charlie nudges Squizzy. 'What do you reckon, boss? She might be his new jockey for the cup.' They both laugh. 'To answer your question, Squizzy, yes, I shall have a horse in the cup. I want the trophy to return to its rightful place, Wombat Springs.' 'On the day, we must have a wager, see if you can get back the money that you lost last year. Well, can't stay gabbing all day, fire her up, Charlie. See you on race day, Ronnie.'

It's Friday, the day before race day, and there is a frenzy of activity at the hotel. Bob and Jack are hanging a large banner up over the stage. It reads: 'ONE NIGHT ONLY. CURLY RIVERS, THE WESTERN PLAINS YODELLER, AND HIS BACKING BAND, THE COCKY-STRANGLERS.' Kat and Sheila are stocking the fridges and setting up tables. Two girls are in the kitchen preparing food. Sheila says to Kat, 'It will be busy tonight. People are starting to arrive for the big day.' It's closing time, and the only car parked outside is the police Land Rover. Inside, Senior Constable Lance Hobbs is helping Kat clean up. They finish and are sitting at the bar. Kat has a rum and coke, and Lance is sipping a shandy. Lance reaches over and takes Kat's hand, raises it to his lips, and gently kisses it. Kat smiles and looks into his eyes. 'I have only known you for a month, but is seems like forever.' 'I know, my love. Well, I had better go. It will be a big day tomorrow.' He kisses her and leaves.

It's the big day, and people have come from miles around. There is a crowd of several hundred. A beer tent is doing a roaring trade. There are food stalls, bookmakers, and market stalls. The ladies are in their finest gowns and hats. Ronald and Beatrice are in the VIP tent. Squizzy approaches them. 'What ho, Ronnie, I've been down to the stables, and I didn't see a horse in your stall. What happened, couldn't you find a jockey to ride your nag?' 'Oh, they will be along before the cup race.' 'In that case, what about a little wager? Shall we say twenty pounds?' 'Why don't we say forty?' Replies Ronald. 'You're on. With my horse and Charlie riding, you are in for a canning.' A voice comes over the loudspeakers. 'Good afternoon, Ladies and Gentlemen. I'm Reg Shoe, and I'll be calling this, the main event of the day. The Wombat Springs Cup, sponsored by the Wombat Springs Hotel. We have a field of nine starters, and the hot favourite is Broadsword owned by Mr Taylor and ridden by Charlie Saddlehorn, last year's winner. Next favourite Danny boy is owned and trained by Mr Weatherby. I don't have the jockey's name.

The green flag is up, and they are off. Reg starts to call the race. Broadsword got a good start, so did Repco Lad. Danny Boy missed the start and is last. Going into the first turn, and Chewing Gum is sticking to the rails. Banana is coming through the bunch, and Bookies Friend has the lead. They are at the halfway mark, and Danny Boy has gained ground and is third behind Broadsword and Repco Lad. Around the turn now, and headed up the straight with two hundred to go, and the whips are out. It's Broadsword from Danny Boy. Danny Boy, Broadsword. Danny Boy kicks on. They hit the line. I give it to Danny Boy, by a head.

Broadsword, second, and Repco Lad third. So the trophy has returned to Wombat Springs. Well done.' Danny Boy and his jockey are led into the enclosure in front of the Grandstand. The jockey dismounts and pulls the bandanna from her face and removes her cap to reveal shoulder-length blonde hair. David is at the front of the crowd. 'Well, blow me down, that's Miss Goodfellow, our teacher.' Ronald embraces her. 'Well done, my dear, and you shall have the winner's prize of fifty Pounds.' 'Why, that's very generous of you, Ronald, thank you.' Charlie comes up to Beatrice and holds out his hand. 'I've never been beaten by a girl before. But you won fair and square, well done, miss.' Squizzy shoulders through the crowd with the chief steward in tow. He loudly proclaims. 'I wish to lodge a protest. She is a woman, and this is not a Ladies event. So this horse should be disqualified.' The chief Steward takes a book from his pocket and waves it at Squizzy. 'There is nothing in here that says a woman can't compete. So the protest is dismissed, the results stand.' There is much cheering from the crowd. For many years after, people would talk about the day that the lady school teacher won the Wombat Springs Cup.

THE END

Halley's Treasure

It was your average spaceport bar, with humanoids and all types of creatures partaking of whatever drug works for them. Swirling lights, weird music, and bar staff that are part reptile, part humanoid. Seeing a topless female humanoid in a short skirt with a scaly tail might arouse some people, but Errol had other things on his mind. Such as what was going to happen when he went to pay, what he suspected, was going to be a rather large bar tab, when he knew that he had no credit left on his star card. The two goons posing as security at the exits didn't look like charitable, unforgiving types. If he came to their attention, he could expect a painful discussion, followed by ejection into the street and a suggestion never to return.

A tall blonde woman leans over the table. She has sparkling blue eyes. She is dressed in space armour, with an empty holster on each hip. She addresses Errol. 'As I live and breathe, if it isn't Errol Starlight. Mind if I join you, what would you like to drink?' 'I never say no to a drink. A golden tonsil tickler would hit the spot.' 'Very good. I'll be right back.' She returns with two drinks. 'There you go.' He raises his glass. 'So where do I know you from?'

She replies. 'It was back in '09. I was a redhead then, but hey, blondes have more fun, right? Anyway, you were one of the security detail guarding a shipment of Kryptonite for the Klingons. We came along and relieved you of the said shipment.' Errol laughs. 'Annette, Queen of the pirates, well, bugger me. I heard that the Klingons had tracked you and your crew down and killed you all.' Annette stands, 'I'll just go and get a couple of more drinks and tell you what happened.' She returns. 'There you go, cheers. The Klingons did indeed come after us. We had a series of fights; they ended up killing all of my crew. I managed to escape and stashed the Kryptonite on a passing comet. Then my ship finally died. I was rescued by a Samaritan ship. What a drag that was, no booze and preaching at me all the time. Man, I was glad to get off that ship.' 'So what happens now? How much is the Kryptonite worth?' Errol asks. 'Well, on the open market, it's worth about ten thousand Credits a block. I have one thousand blocks, so that's ten million less commission.' A woman approaches the table, she pulls out a chair and sits down. She is in her fifties, short and stocky with short dark hair. She is wearing a leather jacket and old jeans. She has a large drink in one hand and a cigar in the corner of her mouth. She removes the cigar and says to Errol, 'That bastard from the Port Authority came back again. He says that unless we pay our overdue docking fees, he's going to impound the ship and kick us off. Where the hell are we going to get two thousand Credits?' Errol does the introductions. 'Annette, this is Tilly, my co-pilot and navigator. Tilly, this is Annette.' Annette and Tilly shake hands. 'Pleased to meet you, Tilly. You sound like a gal after my own heart.' She turns to Errol. 'So you have a ship?' 'I sure do' 'Well, why don't I fix the bar tab and get some takeaways, and we go to your ship. I think that we might be able to do some business.'

They leave the spaceport and take the travel-way along the parking area. There are many ships of different types and makes. Errol steps off the travel-way and walks up to a ship. It is about fifty metres long. It has patches of corrosion, scratches, and dents all over it. Sitting by the main hatchway is a man wearing only shorts and an old hat, alongside of him is a small table. He could be any age between thirty and fifty.

He has red hair and a beard, is thin, and is holding a bottle. Annette looks at the ship. 'Bugger me, isn't this an old mark three Chrysler. I thought that they had all been scrapped years ago, and who's this?' The man in the chair doffs his hat and says, 'My good woman, Spanner at your service. For my sins, I have the job of keeping this ship flying, which I might add, I do very well. At the moment, I'm catching a few rays and enjoying a little vino.' Errol approaches the ship and enters some numbers into a keypad. A door swings open. He turns back to Spanner. 'Spanner, this is Annette, come on inside. I think that she has something to interest us.' 'I can see what she's carrying and she's got my interest.' They follow Errol inside, Annette looks around. 'Yeah, it's an old Chrysler alright.' They go through an airlock. Spanner spreads his arms. 'This is the bridge.' Annette stares. 'What the hell is this? These controls are for a Star Drive and what are these controls for?' 'Those, me darlin', are for a small bank of phasers and anti-laser shields.' Errol interrupts. 'We do the odd job for Arthur Corkscrew, as in say, someone forgets to make the payments on a ship that they have brought from Arthur. He calls us and we track down the ship, and there isn't a ship made that Spanner can't hotwire. As part of the payment, Arthur gives Spanner any little toys that he wants. So, Annette, from what you have told me, you are in the market for a ship and crew.' Annette, Errol, Spanner, and Tilly are gathered around a table in Errol's cabin. They each have a drink. Annette repeats what she has told Errol. Tilly gasps. 'Jesus, you stole that much from the Klingons? How come they haven't caught and killed you?' 'Believe me, they have tried, but as you probably know, the Klingons are brutal and greedy, but luckily, not very bright.' Spanner asks, 'So like, where's the stash now?' 'Well, I took two blocks with me, one of which I have cashed in, the other I still have. The rest I managed to stash on a passing comet that I managed to land on.' Tilly looks impressed. 'Jesus, you managed to land on a comet, that must have been hairy.' Annette nods in agreement. 'Desperate situations call for desperate measures. It was the only way that I could lose the Klingon ship.' 'So where is this comet now?' asks Errol. 'Ah, there we have a bit of a problem. What I have been able to find out is that the comet is called Halley's Comet and that it is due to pass close to old Earth shortly.' 'All right,' says Errol. 'If we go and help you recover this treasure, what's the deal?' 'Well, how I see it is because it's mine, I get fifty percent and the other half is yours.' Spanner interjects, 'Well, how I see it, without us you won't be going anywhere and that being the case, I think that entitles us to equal shares, which after commissions and expenses, should give us about two point two million Credits each and for that, I will take us to hell and back.' Errol adds, 'That goes for Tilly and me. So do we have a deal? Two point two million is a hell of a lot better than bugger all.' 'Okay, okay, we've got a deal. I think that we should start by going to old Earth and finding out about this comet.' Errol stands. 'Right, let's get on it. Tilly, set about plotting a course for old Earth. Spanner, you go with Annette and pay that bastard our mooring fees and get whatever provisions that we need. I'll ask around and see if I can find anyone that has visited old Earth.'

They are ready to leave. Errol calls a meeting on the bridge. 'I talked to a couple of traders that have visited old Earth and apparently it has been declared a Green planet and is protected by a force field, that is controlled by a space station that orbits the planet. Tilly, do we have a course?' 'We do, I've programmed it into the ship's Nav computer.' 'Good. Spanner, are we ready to rock?' 'Good, let's get this show on the road.'

They leave the spaceport and start orbiting the planet in preparation to engage Warp Drive. Errol is in the captain's chair, Tilly is at the Navigators console, Annette is at the comm's desk, and Spanner is in the power plant. Errol to Spanner, 'Okay Spanner, prepare to engage Warp Drive.' Then the ship is rocked violently, and there is a sound of something hitting the ship's hull. The main monitor screen comes to life, displaying a ship's bridge. Reclining in a seat is a humanoid figure with purple scaly skin, a pointed head, and a hand with claws instead of fingers. 'I am Captain Garfront of the Imperial Klingon Navy. We believe that a certain pirate woman is aboard your ship. She has stolen from us. If you teleport her across to our ship, you can be on your way,' Garfront says. Errol speaks. 'I am Captain Errol Starlight, and this is the I.M.S. LEMON. By what right do you attack an unarmed ship?' Garfront replies, 'Because we can. Now hand over that woman. Do not even think about trying to run with your pile of excrement ship.' Spanner's voice comes over the intercom. 'The bastard, I'll show him, when you're ready, skipper.' Errol addresses Garfront. 'I'm afraid I'm going to have to disappoint you, Captain. Goodbye.' 'Spanner, GO.' The ship goes into Warp Drive. Annette is looking at her console. 'My god, according to these readings, we are travelling at warp factor nine. I've never known a ship that could do more than seven. Spanner, what have you done to this ship?' 'I've just hit it with a bigger hammer, darlin'.' It's sometime later and Tilly says, 'Errol, we should be approaching old Earth's solar system.' 'Okay, Tilly. Everyone prepare to come out of Warp Drive. Spanner, on my mark, five, four, three, two, mark.' 'Right, let's see if the Klingons were able to follow us. Anything on the screens, Tilly?' 'No, it looks like we lost them. We are approaching old Earth. I can see where the force field is surrounding the planet; the space station that controls it must be on the other side of the planet.'

They approach the space station, which is more than ten times the size of their ship. It has banks of solar panels. They enter the station's docking bay, and the airtight doors close behind them. A face appears on the ship's monitor. It is a woman in her twenties; she has green hair and a lot of colourful makeup. 'Greetings, my name is Purple Buttercup. This station is currently unmanned. I see from our monitors that you are Earthling descent. This does not allow you to go onto the planet. No one is allowed on Earth. You will be permitted to stay on this station for two days. I suggest that you visit the historian. He will be able to answer any of your questions. Enjoy your stay.'

Annette. 'Right, let's go and see this historian dude and find out when Halley's Comet is due.' They leave the ship and follow the signs to an amphitheatre. As they enter, a large screen lights up. Standing in the centre is an old man with a long white beard, he is wearing a long yellow robe. In the background is a slowly revolving planet Earth.

'Welcome. I am Professor Nigel Frogmarch. I will give you a short history on why the Earth was abandoned. In the twenty-first century, Earth relied on fossil fuels for heating, agriculture, transport, and most other things, including what was needed to build and launch this station. In the twenty-twenties, small groups of people began a push to stop global warming, which they claimed was caused by carbon emissions. To this end, the World Bank and what was then the most powerful country on the planet began offering incentives to become "green". As a result, in a short space of time, power outages and food shortages began happening, even in the rich countries.

This was followed by riots, which led to the food wars of Twenty Thirty. After five years of war, famine, and disease, the survivors decided that their only hope was to combine their remaining resources, build ships, and head for the stars. This they did. The remaining people died out over the next two hundred years. You are descendants of the people that left. You may ask any questions that you have.' Annette asks, 'What do you know of Halley's Comet? Can you tell us when it is due to pass Earth?' Nigel answers, 'The head of the comet is roughly eight kilometres long and two kilometres wide. It has a rocky surface with small hills and one crater. Its surface temperature is between minus twenty degrees Celsius and minus one hundred and three degrees Celsius.' Annette exclaims, 'That's it. That's where I left it, in that crater.' Nigel continues, 'The comet is due to pass Earth in twenty of our days. It will be travelling at thirty-seven thousand miles an hour. It should be visible in ten days' time.' Tilly asks, 'How the hell are we supposed to land on that, and then go out in those temperatures and recover the goodies?' 'Well, I did it, admittedly I had no choice, I had to escape the Klingons. Any half decent space suit will handle the temperatures. The ones that you have on board will be fine.' Annette responds. Errol asks Spanner, 'What do you reckon of our chances of landing without wrecking the ship?' 'You are the best pilot that I know and with Tilly to help, we should manage. Annette, was there a lot of turbulence as you came into land?' 'It was a bit rough on the way in, but it was fine once I landed, especially once I was in the crater,' Annette recalls. Errol addresses them, 'Okay, we will stay here for the next two days and make sure that we are ready. Spanner, have a look around and see if you can find anything that might be useful.' Two days later, they are preparing to leave. Spanner approaches Errol. 'Skipper, I've found something that could be very useful. It's an anti-grav all-terrain forklift. It will be ideal for carting the Kryptonite to the ship.' 'Well done. Space station control, this is the I.M.S. Lemon requesting permission to leave.' The same woman appears on the screen. 'Wait just one minute, our monitors show that you have a piece of our equipment on your ship. The airlock will remain closed until it is returned. You may also face a penalty.' Spanner appears on the bridge and sits at a console. He turns to Errol. 'Crank her up, Skipper, I'll have those doors open in two minutes.' Errol starts the ship and slowly rotates until they are facing the doors. They open. The woman shouts, 'What do you think you are doing? I order you to stop. What you are doing is illegal.' Errol answers, 'Mate, where we come from illegal is a sick bird, bye.' It's days later and the comet fills their monitor screens.

Errol comes on the intercom. 'Is everyone strapped in? Good. Here we go.'

The ship is rocking violently, alarms are sounding. Errol shouts. 'Tilly, the autopilot can't handle it. I'm going to manual. I need you to give me course and distance.' 'On it, Skipper, keep to the heading you're on. Range three kilometres and closing. Spanner, more power, that's good. Two kilometres... One, back off the power, looking good. We're going in, prepare to land.' Sounds of bangs and thumps, then silence. Annette is the first on her feet. 'Well done everyone, bloody marvellous. When I left the stash here, I also left a beacon with it, now let's see if it is still working. WOO, HOO. Here it is just under a kilometre to the north of us.' Errol says, 'Great. Spanner, Annette, and I will suit up and go get the goodies. Tilly, you stay and monitor the comms in case we run into any trouble.'

It's been some four hours since they have left the comet, and the crew are having a victory party on the bridge. Errol asks Annette, 'So where do we go to sell this stuff?'

'We go to the planet Virgin, in the Meldrum Solar system. I know a guy there that will take it off our hands for cash. That's where I was headed before. Tilly, could you program that into the nav computer?' 'Sure thing. There we go. Done.' Errol goes to the captain's chair. 'Okay, Spanner, warp factor five, let's go.'

Errol is in the same station bar that he was a year ago. He is grinning happily to himself. He senses movement and looks across the table. Annette stands there with a glass in each hand, she says, 'Well howdy stranger, there you go, a Golden Tonsil Tickler.' 'Annie, great to see you. How did you find me?' 'It wasn't hard, I just followed the trail of pissed off women and empty bottles. How much of the two million do you have left?' 'Probably enough to pay the bar tab and the mooring fees. I was never much good at holding onto money.' 'What about Tilly and Spanner?' 'Tilly hooked up with a guy from the planet Zog, they bought some kind of ranch there. Spanner found a way to get to old Earth and is happily tinkering away there. What about you?' 'Well, I like to get it but, like you, I'm not much good at keeping it. So, you still have your ship?' 'I sure do, why, do you have something in mind?' 'Well, it just so happens.'

THE END

Harold The Bandit

The kingdom of Abel is a small Island nation. Its main sources of income are from tourism and spaghetti exports. It is governed by King Bruce and Queen Shiela. They have a son, Chuck, and a daughter, Porsha. It is morning, and Bruce and Shiela are having breakfast in the dining room. Bruce is reading the local paper, the Abel Bugle.

Chuck and Porsha enter. Chuck is in his thirties, medium height with a slight paunch and dark hair, he is dressed in a dark suit and tie. Porsha is in her twenties, attractive with blonde hair and a slim figure. She is wearing red slacks with a matching top.

Chuck, in a rather posh slightly nasal voice asks, 'What ho, what wonders has Mrs Carbunkle dished up today? Bruce looks up from his paper, 'Good morning, Chuck, Porsha. There are devilled kidneys, lamb's fry, bacon, and toast.' Chuck approaches the table, 'Jolly good, just the ticket.' Porsha turns up her nose, 'Ugh, why don't we ever have real food, cereal, fruit, or tofu?' 'I'm afraid that you will have to take that up with Mrs Carbunkle,' replies Shiela. 'Anything interesting in the paper, dear?'

'Well, the main story seems to be about the Golden Pyramid Bank. It seems that the board have approved some dodgy loans to people who have either disappeared, or have no assets. To make matters worse, they tried to cover it up by using their Super Funds and have lost even more.' Chuck says. 'I say, I was offered a position on the board of Golden Pyramid.' Bruce scoffs. 'What. You! I would have thought that one would have to have some knowledge of fiscal policy to be offered a position like that.' 'Oh no, one just has to be one of the chaps, don't ya know,' Chuck retorts. Shiela looks at Bruce, 'All that I can say is that I'm glad that our finances are in the hands of a trustworthy institute. I could never trust that Ian Deeppockets.' 'You mean SIR Ian Deeppockets, chairman of the board, my dear,' Bruce corrects. It's a cold, wet, Friday afternoon in the town of Dunrootin. A man is sheltering under the porch of a closed shop. He is medium height, slim, wearing a long dark coat with a cap pulled down, hiding most of his face. Across the road is a branch of the Golden Pyramid bank. He crosses the road and enters. Once in the bank, he looks around. It appears to be deserted. He approaches the counter. Suddenly, the face of a woman appears from below the counter. She is attractive in her forties with blonde curly hair, blue eyes, and a nice smile. She says, 'Hello, terrible day.' He pulls a gun out from under his coat and points it at the ceiling, shouting, 'This is a stick-up! Who else is here?' 'Well, I never. I'm the only one here. Old Mr Magoo, the manager, and the teller go to the pub on Friday afternoons and leave me to lock up. So, I suppose you'll be wanting all the money?' she responds. 'That's right, and no tricks or I will have to use this,' he says, waving the gun. The woman replies, 'Listen, dear, my dad had me shooting rabbits and pheasants when I was ten years old. That silly little .410 that you've got there won't do much damage. Now did you bring a bag for the money?' He replies sheepishly, 'Er, no, do you have one?' She says, 'Sure, wait a mo' and I'll go and empty the safe.' She goes out the back and returns with a bulging bag, which she hands to the man. 'There you go, now, I'll just go and get my hat and coat and we can be on our way.' Startled, he says, 'What, you can't come with me? After this, I'll be an outlaw, on the run.'

'Listen to me. I'm a forty-something spinster, living in a small town. The best that I can look forward to is a pension in about twenty years and living in a house with cats. This will likely be my only chance to escape, now let's go.'

They leave the bank, and he leads her around the corner and they get into a black Ford coupe. They are seated in the car; he turns to her and holds out a hand. 'I suppose I should introduce myself, I'm Harold.' 'Pleased to meet you, Harold, I'm Molly. Would you mind if we called into home so that I can get some things? It's only ten minutes away.' 'Sure thing. I must say, this is rather different to what I thought bank robbing would be like.' They drive off and pull up outside a small stone cottage. Molly gets out. 'I'll be as quick as I can.' Molly enters the house and goes down a passageway to a small kitchen. An elderly woman is sitting at a table; she looks up as Molly enters. 'You're early, dear.' 'Yes, Mum, my friend and I have just robbed the bank. I'll just go up and get some things.' Molly goes upstairs and returns with a small suitcase. 'Are you going somewhere, dear?' Yes, Mum. 'We will be on the run; the police will be here on Monday. I'll call you when I can.' But, dear, 'it's Friday night; Bert Entwhisle will be here to take you down to the darts at the Slaughtered Goat.' Molly replies, 'Another good reason to leave.' 'Oh well, if you're sure, dear. Here's a nice cottage pie and a couple of bottles of ale to take.' 'Thanks, Mum. See ya.' Molly gives her mum a hug and a kiss and leaves through the front door. As they drive away, Molly's mum thinks, who would have thought, my little girl, a gangster's moll. Harold and Molly drive for about an hour, then drive down a country lane and turn into an overgrown driveway. They drive down a rutted track and come to an old farmhouse. Harold drives around the back and parks in an old barn. Harold leads the way; they enter through the rear door. 'Here we are, there's no power but I have lamps. If you would like to freshen up, there's a bathroom and toilet through that door; I'll get the stove going.'

It's sometime later; the stove is glowing. Molly and Harold are sitting at a table in a large kitchen. It is barely furnished; there is a bed made up against one wall. They are eating cottage pie and each have a glass of ale. Molly looks at Harold. 'Well, this is cosy. Who owns this place?' 'It was my father's; he owned it freehold. I had been working for Golden Pyramid for years when the manager suggested that Dad should buy shares in the bank, that way he would have a comfortable retirement. I thought that it would be a great idea as well. All was good until a few months ago when shares in the bank crashed.' 'Yes, I remember. A lot of small investors lost everything. So what happened to your dad?' 'The bank foreclosed, sold off the stock and machinery. Dad was devastated and ended up in a nursing home. I suppose that the council will eventually sell up the place to cover back rates.' 'That is so sad. It's always the little people that get hurt. You weren't able to help?' 'I planned to. I took a redundancy and planned to use my superannuation to pay off the debts, but then I found out that the bank had used the superannuation funds to pay off their debts, so I had bugger all. That's when I decided to get what they owed me. So I did some planning and today was the beginning.' 'Well, it was a pretty good start. I figure that we have about twelve thousand dollars. What are we going to do with it?' 'I have a plan.' A Hardley Normal van pulls up outside of the One Foot In The Grave nursing home. The driver approaches reception. The nurse at the counter asks, 'Can I help you?' 'I have a large screen television and Karaoke machine to deliver and install.'

The nurse replies, 'Are you sure? We haven't ordered anything, and I don't think that the owners would buy those things.' The driver looks at his notes. 'This is the place; it's all been paid for. Let's see, ah yes, by a Mister Edward Kelly.' 'Well, what a lovely surprise! We can certainly use the television, and the Karaoke machine will be great on singalong nights.' It's night; a limousine is speeding along a country road when it comes to a screeching halt. A voice in the rear yells, 'Jones, what the hell are you playing at?' The driver replies, 'I'm sorry, Sir Ian, there seems to be a tree across the road.' Before Sir Ian can reply, a car pulls up behind them, its lights on high beam. The driver's door is yanked open to reveal a masked figure holding a pistol. A woman's voice says, 'Now, you are only the driver, no need for heroics. Hand over that pistol that you're wearing, and there won't be any trouble.' The rear door is likewise opened to also reveal a masked gunman. The gunman, in a pleasant voice, says. 'Good evening, Sir Ian, on your way to your weekly card game, I see. Now, I'll just take this little brown bag here, and we'll be on our way.' Sir Ian yells, 'How dare you! I'll see you both in jail for life, you swine.' From the front of the car comes the sound of smashing glass, and the headlights go out. The gunman speaks, 'Well, Sir Ian, you may be a bit late and a bit poorer, but you can still make your card game. We bid you goodnight.' Sir Ian yells, 'Don't think for a minute that you will get away with this! I'll have every policeman in the land after you.' The door slams shut, the car behind revs up, and speeds into the night.

King Bruce is in his office at the castle. Jeeves, the butler, shows in Sir Ian, who approaches Bruce's desk. 'Now listen here, Bruce, you need to do something about this.' Bruce looks up and says coldly, 'First of all, it's King Bruce or Sire to you, and secondly, just what is it that you want something done about?' 'Of course, forgive me, Sire, it's just that these bank robberies make one jolly angry. Two of our branches have been hit in the last month.' 'Yes, one wonders why it is only the Golden Pyramid bank that seems to be targeted.' 'I'm sure that it is only a matter of time before other banks suffer the same fate. The board has asked me to see you and ask what you are doing about this band of cutthroats.' Bruce replies, 'I haven't heard of any throats being cut. In answer to your question, the next person that I am seeing is the officer in charge of the case. Don't let me detain you any longer.' A policeman in uniform is shown in. 'Ah, Sergeant Plod, how goes it with what I understand the press are calling the Harold the bandit robberies?' 'Sire, we now know the identities of the perpetrators, a woman by the name of Molly Gizzard and Harold Fargone, both ex-employees of the Golden Pyramid bank. Now that we know their identities, it is only a matter of time before we apprehend them.' 'One hopes, sooner rather than later, Sergeant, keep me informed.'

An Acme Mobility Scooter van pulls up outside the Golden Years retirement home. The driver goes to reception and speaks to the sister on duty. 'I have six mobility scooters, charged and ready to go.' The sister is clearly surprised, 'There must be some mistake, the board would never agree to that sort of expense.' The driver replies, 'Says here that they have been paid for by a mister Robin Hood. Now where would you like them?'

'In the foyer, please. Oh, this is better than Christmas.'

It's a windy, wet Friday afternoon, and Sergeant Plod is in a police car, parked in an alley across from a Golden Pyramid bank. A constable is behind the wheel. Sergeant Plod says to the Constable, 'Be ready, Jones, so far the bandits have always struck on a Friday. I've got other cars on the lookout, if they try it on we'll have 'em.' The police radio crackles into life. 'Base to Sergeant Plod, come in, over.' 'Plod to base, go ahead.' 'The bank in Threadcotton Street has just been done over, suspects are in a black coupe.' Just then a black coupe roars past the alley. Sergeant plod yells at the driver, 'There they go, after them, put your foot down.' The police car swerves into the street siren and lights on. The police car comes to the main road that leads out of town. Plod is excited, 'Now which way did they go? There they are going over that crest, left man, after them, I've got them now.' The road goes from Bitumen to gravel, the police car is gaining. The constable is enjoying the chase, they come out of a left-hand corner in a nice controlled slide when fifty yards ahead a farm tractor comes out of a farm gate into the road. The constable swings the wheel; they fly off the road into a muddy dam. The car disappears behind a wall of muddy water. It clears to reveal the police car with water halfway up its doors. Sergeant Plod staggers out and bangs his fists on the car in frustration, 'BUGGER, BUGGER.' Meanwhile, Harold and Molly are driving down a country lane. They come to the end of the lane, which ends at a boat ramp and a small jetty. Tied up at the jetty is a small ketch. Harold parks at the top of the boat ramp. Harold turns to Molly, 'Here we are, my love, what do you think of our boat?' 'Oh, Harold, it's lovely.' 'Alright then, you start loading our gear onto the boat, and I'll take care of the car.' Once the gear is out of the car, Harold leans in, releases the handbrake, and the car rolls down the ramp into the water. It floats for a couple of minutes and then sinks beneath the waves. Harold joins Molly on the boat. 'Alright, love, you let go the lines, then once we get into open water, you can take the wheel and I will hoist the sails. With luck and a fair wind, we should get to the big Island in five days.' Molly gives him a kiss. 'Once we get there I think we should open a little shop.' 'That sounds great, love.'

As the yacht sails away, the last rays of the setting sun highlight the name on the stern: WITHDRAWAL TWO.

THE END

The Voyage of The Empire Rose

A woman walks along the jetty. She is tall, rather slim with long chestnut hair. She is wearing a long dark skirt with a white blouse and a green jacket. She is looking at a ship that is tied up to the jetty. It is a 20-metre twin mast schooner with a clipper bow and nice lines, but it has seen better days. The once-white hull is a dirty grey, the cabin and rails are in need of varnish, and the sails that are furled on the booms are dirty and patched. She walks the length of the ship and looks at the name on the stern. Faded gold letters read Empire Rose. She walks up the gangway and steps lightly onto the deck. There is a hammock slung between the mast and the rail, underneath it is an empty rum bottle. She gives the hammock a kick with her boot. A bleary face with bloodshot eyes peers over the edge of the hammock. 'What the blood—Oh hello, Miss.' 'It's not Miss, it's lady to you. I'm looking for Captain Horatio Bumhole. Who might you be?' 'I'm Master Bates, the first mate, your lady. The Captain will be in his cabin, I'll show you the way.'

They descend down the companionway, along a passageway, to a cabin door. Master Bates knocks. 'There is a lady to see you, Cap'n.' A voice comes from the cabin. 'If it's Saucey Sue from the tavern, I'm not interested.' 'No, Cap'n, it's a real lady.'

'Very well, give me a couple of minutes.' 'Very well, you may enter.'

Master Bates shows the lady into the cabin and leaves. The cabin is spacious, with a large bunk against one wall, a table and chairs, and a desk behind which stands a man. He is medium height, well-built with dark hair, greying at the temples, he has blue eyes and a gold earring in his left ear. He gives a slight bow. 'Captain Horatio Bumhole at your service, ma'am.'

The lady replies, 'Captain, my name is Lady Anne Fingerbottom.'

'Would that be the same Fingerbottom that owns the To and Fro Ferry Services?' he asks.

'That is correct, Captain. The reason that I am here is that I wish to charter you and your ship, Captain. I have asked around and you have made several trips to the Unfriendly Islands.'

'Yes, that is true. I am familiar with those islands, but why would you wish to charter the Rose? Surely you have your own ships and crews?'

'That's true,' she replies, 'but our ships are coastal, not ocean-going. The one exception is the reason that I am here. For two months, I was bedridden with the Cortina fever, and while I was in this state, someone got into my useless husband's ear with tales of an island where gold can be picked up off the ground. Whoever it was must have been convincing because my stupid husband sailed off in our schooner. As far as I am concerned, I would be happy if he never returned, but he has our only child, my fifteen-year-old daughter, with him.

She has always idolised him. He filled her head with tales of exotic places and brave deeds, most of which he picked up from the waterfront taverns where he spent most of his time.'

'Ah yes,' says Horatio with a smile, 'gold can have a powerful effect on some people.'

'Captain, I wish to charter your ship to find my lousy husband and, more importantly, to find my daughter. How many crew do you have?'

Horatio looks thoughtful. 'Ah yes, crew. Now, opinion is divided on that.'

Anne looks puzzled. 'What do you mean?'

Horatio replies, 'Well, some captains say that you need them, but I say that you don't. Let's say that you hire a crew. First, you have to feed them. Then let's say that you have been at sea for four months and things are not going well. The crew are likely to mutiny, cut your throat, and sail off with your ship.'

They are interrupted by a knocking on the cabin door. The door opens and an elderly Chinese man enters. He is perhaps five feet tall with a ponytail down his back. He is carrying a tray, he bows and puts the tray on the table.

He speaks with an accent. 'Coffee and cake for Missee?'

'Lady Anne, this is Lee Chew, our cook. Lee, this is Miss Anne, she maybe charter ship.'

Lee bows to Anne. 'That would be good, maybe we get some good chow.' He bows and leaves. Anne resumes, 'So tell me, Captain, how do you sail without a crew?' 'Well,' explains Horatio, 'a friend of mine has a farm and three strapping sons that he has little work for. They are happy to get away from the farm and make some money. With them, Master Bates, and myself, we manage.'

'So, Captain, to business, here are ten gold sovereigns to cover the refit and new sails, and here are some silver pieces to cover ongoing costs.'

Horatio looks at the money Anne has put on his desk. 'Yes, my word, that should cover it. Let's say five weeks for the refit, another week for provisions. We should be ready to sail in about seven weeks.'

Anne shakes her head. 'Not in seven weeks, Captain. Tomorrow morning, I will have my best shipwright here. We will sail in three weeks.'

'We? What do you mean, WE?' Horatio asks. Anne replies, 'Of course, I shall be coming.'

Horatio shakes his head. 'Out of the question. We are not equipped to have a woman on board, especially a lady like yourself.' 'Captain, I have been aboard boats and ships since I was six years old. I shall use the first mate's cabin. I am sure that for a few shillings extra he will not mind sharing with the crew. Now, Captain, do we have a deal?' 'That we do, Lady Anne. So, how do we find this husband of yours?' Anne replies, 'One of my officers overheard them talking the night before they left. They were heading for the Unfriendly Island and then turning South.'

They return to the deck, where Horatio bids her good day and returns to his cabin. As the mate leads her to the gangway, they pass a bundle of orange fur on top of a keg. Anne reaches out to pat it.

A sinewy arm extends, a paw opens, and razor-sharp claws appear. Anne quickly withdraws her hand. Master Bates says, 'I wouldn't do that, Lady. That's Twinkles, the ship's cat. The way he sees the world is that if he can't eat it, fight it, or make love to it, he doesn't want to know. The only person that can touch him is Lee Chew.'

It is two weeks later, and the Empire Rose has been transformed. Her hull is gleaming white, the topsides have been varnished, and new sails are on her booms. Lady Anne comes aboard followed by two workers with two sea chests. Master Bates greets her. 'Welcome aboard, my lady. Your cabin is ready. We will be sailing with the tide.' Horatio comes on deck and mans the wheel. 'Mr Bates, cast off fore and aft, hoist the foresail.' They sail down the river and enter the open sea. It is a glorious morning with a northerly breeze. Anne joins him. 'So, Captain, how long will it take us to reach the Unfriendly Islands?' Horatio looks at her. 'Now that we are at sea, why don't you call me Horatio? And to answer your question, with good weather, it should take about two weeks.' She replies, 'Thank you, Horatio. And when we are alone, you may call me Anne.'

They have been at sea for a week. It is late afternoon, black clouds are forming, and the wind is picking up. Master Bates approaches the helm. 'Captain, the glass has dropped to buggery. I reckon that we are in for a blow.' 'Yeah,' Horatio replies, 'I'd say that we have about an hour. It'll be on us about dark. Batten the hatches, have Lee secure the galley, furl the sails, and hoist the storm jib.'

It is almost dark. Horatio is at the wheel, the seas are rising, and the wind is howling through the rigging. A figure in oilskins is making its way along the deck and reaches the wheel. 'Anne, what the hell are you doing here? We're in for a bad blow; you should be below.' Horatio exclaims. Anne replies, 'What and let you have all the fun? I want to see how good a sailor you are. I'll help with the helm.' It's dark, the sea lit by flashes of lightning, the wind hurls rain across the deck. The Rose streaks down the face of the waves, coming through the crests in a cloud of spray. Anne and Horatio fight the wheel, hair streaming in the wind, both shouting with excitement. An hour later, and the storm has gone as quickly as it came. The wind has died, and only a mild swell remains. Master Bates approaches. 'Well done, you two. I'll take over now, Go below and dry off.'

They are in Horatio's cabin. Horatio hands Anne a dry towel. 'Would you like a brandy?' 'Oh, my word, yes. You know, I haven't felt that alive in years.' Anne responds. Horatio looks at her. 'That was the first time that I have heard you laugh, and it was glorious.' They are sitting on Horatio's bed, wrapped in a blanket, sipping brandy, laughing. His hand touches hers, they kiss.

It is ten days later and the Empire Rose is at anchor in a wide bay. Lush green vegetation covers the low hills, white sandy beaches separate the trees from the crystal-clear water, and there is a small jetty.

Anne and Horatio are leaning on the ship's rail. 'Oh, Horatio, what a beautiful place. I shall go ashore with Lee and get some fresh food.' Anne declares. Horatio nods. 'And I will go and see a mate of mine who has a little tavern and see if he knows anything about your husband.' Anne, Horatio, and Lee get into the Jolly boat. As they prepare to push off, Twinkles nimbly jumps aboard, gouges some grooves in the woodwork with his claws, then leaps onto Lee's lap and drapes over his legs. Lee strokes the cat and says, 'Nice pussy cat, him go ashore, make um, more kitties.' They beach the boat. Horatio says, 'Alright, I'll go to the tavern. Meet you both back here in an hour.' They reconvene at the boat, and Horatio starts to row back to the ship. He says to Anne, 'Well, we are in luck. One of the crew from your husband's ship fell in lust with a local girl and jumped ship. Apparently, they're heading for a small island about one hundred and twenty miles southwest of here. We should be able to find it because it has an active volcano.' Anne asks, 'Did he say anything about my daughter Elizabeth?'

'Yes, she is well, but not enjoying the realities of shipboard life.'

It's a few days later, and they have found the island. They sail into a small bay. There is a village of huts amongst the trees, with canoes drawn up on the beach. A ship is at anchor. 'Horatio, that's our ship, the Lady Ann. It looks deserted. Look, a canoe is coming.' Anne observes. A canoe comes alongside. In it are two natives and a tall, thin lady dressed in a long black dress with a wide-brimmed hat. They help her aboard. She introduces herself. 'Good morning, I'm Sister Mary from the Order of the Black Garter. I'm a missionary. I was sent here to convert the natives. I have been here for nearly twenty years, and I am fluent in their language.' 'Pleased to meet you, Sister. I am Captain Horatio Bumhole, and this is Lady Anne Fingerbottom. We are looking for Anne's daughter, Elizabeth.' Horatio says. Sister Mary looks at Anne. 'So your husband is Randolph Fingerbottom?' Anne frowns. 'Only until I can get a divorce. What of my daughter, Elizabeth?' Sister Mary shakes her head. 'Oh dear. For some reason, there is a lot of gold in the hills here, and your husband heard about it. He arrived here with things to trade—knives, axes, and trinkets. The king traded some gold, but your husband knew that there was much more. Then the king became obsessed with your daughter. The king was going to take her by force, but I managed to intervene. But it's not all good news, I'm afraid. The king offered your husband a goldmine of his own for your daughter, and when your husband saw the mine, he agreed. The king is going to marry your daughter in two days' time.' Mary explains. Anne looks to Mary. 'I must see her. Do you know where she is?' Mary replies, 'If you come with me, I will take you to her.' They go in the canoe and land on the beach. They walk through the village to a hut near the bush, a warrior with a spear is outside. Sister Mary speaks to the warrior who opens the door. Sister Mary speaks into the hut. 'Elizabeth, it's me. I have someone here to see you.' A young girl emerges from the hut. She is tall and attractive. On seeing Anne, she rushes forward and embraces her. 'Oh mother, I'm so glad that you are here. I've missed you so. Father has gone insane. All he can talk about is gold. He doesn't care that I have to marry that repulsive old man. Mother, you must save me.' Anne looks at her daughter. 'Don't worry, love. We will get you out of here. Be ready tonight when the moon is up.' As they walk back through the village, they pass a wooden structure on which hangs a gold disc about two feet in diameter. Anne gasps. 'My god, is that real gold?' 'Yes,' replies Mary. 'They use it to summon the people.' Horatio, Anne, and the crew spend the afternoon making plans. That night, once the moon is up, two boats leave the Rose. One lands to the South of the village and one to the North. Anne gets out of this boat, Lee hands her a box. Inside is a very angry pussy cat. Sister Mary appears out of the shadows. 'Follow me.' They skirt the village. Sister Mary approaches the guard with the box. He motions to open it. Anne lifts the lid, and the guard leans forward. A flying, hissing, orange feline wraps itself around the guard's face and sinks its teeth into a convenient ear. The guard drops his spear and tries to remove the monster. Anne steps behind him and brings a club down on his head. He sinks to the ground with a moan. Anne opens the hut door. 'Elizabeth, come quickly!' Elizabeth rushes out of the hut and embraces Anne. 'Oh mother, I'm so glad that you came. I had almost given up.' Sister Mary whispers, 'Quickly, follow me. We must get back to the boat.' 'I must come with you. I must get away from this place. I have a bag by the boat.' Anne says to her. 'Of course you must come with us. Let's go.'

They are all back on board. The anchor is raised, and sails hoisted. They head out to sea. Anne introduces Elizabeth to Horatio. 'Elizabeth, this is Horatio. We shall be married as soon as I can arrange a divorce.' 'Horatio, what if they come after us?' Elizabeth asks. 'I don't think so, my dear. We cut their anchor cable. She will drift onto the beach. Come, let me show you something.' He leads them down to his cabin and pulls a blanket off something on his table. Elizabeth cries, 'It's the big gold disc!' Horatio replies, 'That's right, my dear. I couldn't just leave it there. This should give the crew a nice bonus, a donation to Sister Mary, and a nice wedding present for us.' Later, Anne, Horatio, and Elizabeth stand at the forward rail, looking at the moonlit sea. Horatio puts his arms around them and says, 'Well, my loves, the world is our mollusc.' The Empire Rose sails off into the moonlight.

THE END

The Travels of Squirrel Little Bottom

As she travelled along the travel-way towards customs, she looked at her reflection in the wall mirrors. The reflections showed that she was human, female, and tall, with a body that most males of her species found attractive. She had spiked red hair and was wearing a long dark coat with cargo pants. On her back, she carried a small pack. From her coat, she takes a small handheld device. It is a Compupanion, given to her by her parents on her eighteenth birthday. She turns it on. 'Well, Pluto, what can you tell me about this place?'

A soft feminine voice issues from the device. 'Just give me a moment to plug into a computer. Ah, here we are. This is the space port Alpha. It has three portals, so you can travel to most of the known universe from here. We are orbiting the planet Finch, which has a population of about two billion.' 'Okay, let's see how we get on with customs. I will insert an earpiece so that you can translate.' She approaches the customs area. In front of her is a booth that contains a creature covered in purple hair. It has two vision censors on stalks on its head. It holds out an arm which ends in a two-fingered claw. Its voice is automatically translated by Pluto.

'I.D. and credit chip.' Squirrel hands over both. Customs scans both. 'I see that you are human. We see very few of you here. Are you transferring or visiting our planet?' 'I would like to visit your planet. Is the atmosphere suitable for humans?' 'Yes. Would you like me to exchange the credits on your chip to our currency? Which is called Fondu. The current exchange rate is twenty credits to one Fondu. This will give you ten Fondu, only just enough to enter our planet. You will have to check in with customs in seven of our days. Teleports to the surface are just down the hall. Enjoy your stay.' Squirrel teleports down to the surface and arrives in the city of Wahoo. It appears to be early evening. Air-cars are flying between buildings. Finchens are out on travel-ways, skyscrapers tower up into the night sky. Squirrel takes out Pluto. 'Okay, Pluto, the first order of business is to find somewhere that I can get a meal, I'm starving.' Pluto answers, 'I think that I have got somewhere. At the next intersection, take the travel-way to your right. Then after about ten minutes, we should come to a place where there are humans.' After about ten minutes, this part of the city begins to change. There are fewer Finchens and more alien beings. The streets are narrower. The shop fronts now advertise bars and houses of negotiable affection. Then, across the street, she sees a hologram above the entrance to a building. In shimmering letters, it says: BAR AND GRILL. 'That looks like us. If we're lucky, it might be run by humans.'

They enter. It is a long, dimly lit room with a bar down one side and booths down the other. At the rear is a small stage with tables and chairs. There are maybe six other humanoids in the place. Behind the bar is a human woman. She is in her late thirties, tall, attractive, with long blonde hair. Squirrel approaches. 'Well, howdy! You must be new in town. I'm Annette, and this is my place. What can I get you?' 'Pleased to meet you. I'm Squirrel. What's on the menu? And a beer would be great.' 'Well, I can do you a sleb burger with salad and fries. There's your beer.' 'The salad and fries for sure, but what exactly is a sleb burger?' 'Frankly, my dear, I've never been game to ask. It comes prepacked, and we cook it on a grill. It's not bad. We eat it.' Just then, the door opens, and in comes a human male. He is stocky, muscular, with long black hair. He is wearing a leather jacket with an open white shirt and black pants. He goes around the bar, puts his arm around Annette, and nibbles her ear.

Annette kisses him. 'Now, now dear, not in front of the customers. Squirrel, this is Errol, my lover and partner. Errol, this is Squirrel. She has just arrived. I'm just going to get her a burger. Would you like one?' 'Sure, honey.' Annette goes out the back. Errol asks, 'I'm getting a drink, would you like another?' It's two hours later, and Annette, Errol, and Squirrel are sitting in a booth. They are laughing, drinking, and telling stories. The bar has been switched to auto-serve. Errol asks Squirrel, 'So, Squirrel, how come you are in our part of the universe? For one so young, you seem well-travelled.' 'I was born on a small planet at the far end of the Milky Way Galaxy. My parents were biologists. They were trying to recreate some of the creatures that used to live on old Earth using DNA. Just before I was born, they had their first success. It was a small furry animal that used to be called a Squirrel, which is how I got my name. When I was seventeen, my parents were trying to recapture a Bug Beast when it turned on them. They both died.' Annette touches her hand. 'That must have been hard. Do you have any siblings?' 'No, I was an only child. I went off the rails for a while—drugs, sex, and booze—but thanks to my parents, Pluto saved me.' Errol asks, 'Pluto, what's a Pluto?' 'This is Pluto. My parents had arranged for me to receive her on my eighteenth birthday.' She takes out Pluto and sits it on the table. 'Pluto, meet Annette and Errol.' Pluto emits a small green beam, which passes over Annette and Errol. Pluto speaks. 'Ah, fellow humans, I see that you have a warmth for Squirrel. That is good' Squirrel explains, 'Pluto is a very advanced computer with AI. She connects only with me.' Errol says, 'Very impressive. So what made you leave your planet, and how did you end up here?' 'My parents had a board to help them run the zoo. After they died, the board turned the zoo into a corporation and then wanted to sell it, and more importantly, the research that my parents had pioneered, making themselves very rich. But unfortunately for them, my parents had left a will stating that nothing could be sold without my permission.' 'So what happened?' 'Oh, they tried threats and bribes, but luckily I had Pluto. On our planet, we have people called lawyers. By legal means, these people could get my zoo back, but they are also very expensive—in this case, about fifty thousand credits. I had very little money, so I took a stash from the zoo and hit the road.' Annette says, 'So I take it that you are trying to raise fifty thousand credits. How do you plan to get that amount of credits?' Squirrel replies, 'In the beginning, I fell in with a couple of grifters and con men. They taught me some tricks. Then, with the help of Pluto, I started boosting air-cars on commission, but Pluto realised that it was too dangerous. For the last two years, I've been working at one of the many casinos on the planet Jackpot. We were in the process of setting up a scam that would have netted me about ten thousand credits when we were busted. We just made it out of there, and here I am.' Annette asks, 'So how much have you raised so far?' 'Just under twenty thousand, and I'm starting to get desperate.' Errol yawns, 'Well, it's getting late. Do you have anywhere to stay?' 'No, well, we have a spare unit out the back. You're welcome to stay, and over breakfast tomorrow, we might have some suggestions.' 'That would be great, thanks.'

It's the next morning, and the three of them are having breakfast by the pool. Errol begins. 'Last night Annie and I got talking. To be honest, we are getting bored with this place, and it only breaks even. How would we go about turning this place into a casino?' 'Well, I would suggest a club rather than a casino. All we would need is a roulette wheel, some blackjack tables, and a cash cow computer and screen.'

Annette says, 'Roulette and blackjack, I know, but what's cash cow?' 'The best money maker of them all. It's a slang name for Electronic Wheel Of Fortune. On the screen is a big wheel with numbers one to forty on it. You can choose up to ten numbers. Each spin will show a number. There are ten spins to a game. If you pick all ten numbers, you win the jackpot. You can also choose lesser numbers for lesser prizes. Best of all, it is all automatic. The punters swipe their card for as many numbers as they want. If they win, the computer pays out in credits, and if they lose, the computer puts the credits into your account.' Errol looks at Annette. 'How about Squirrel gives us a hand with the bar today while we look into what's involved, and we talk it over this evening over dinner?' Both the girls agree. After a busy day, the trio are once again seated by the pool. Squirrel begins. 'I put Pluto on the job to enquire about getting what we need. Tell them what you found, Pluto.' 'I found a company called Acme Gambling Supplies in Logan, which is a large city on this planet. They can supply and deliver everything that you will need for two thousand credits.' Errol says, 'Annie and I talked about this, and we figure that the Reno' on the bar would cost about four thousand credits. So let's say that we can set up for six thousand credits. How much do you think that we will make in, say, a month?' 'I have only been on this planet for a couple of days, so I'm not really sure. But for instance, where I was before, a similar setup would bring in about two thousand credits a night, at least.' Annette is making notes. 'So, how does this sound? We each put in two thousand credits and go thirds in the profits. I have just one more question. Who do we get to deal the cards and spin the wheel?' Squirrel says, 'I think that I can help there. Up on the space port, there will be human hitchhikers. I will find, say, ten. Is there somewhere that we can accommodate them?' Errol says, 'I should be able to find somewhere nearby to lease. I'll get on it tomorrow. So do we have a deal?' The girls agree enthusiastically.

It's sometime later, and the hologram above the entrance now reads ACE OF DIAMONDS. There is a queue lined up to enter. Annette, Errol, and Squirrel are in the office at the rear of the club celebrating the club's first month. Annette hands Squirrel a credit chip. 'Here you go, eight thousand credits, your share for this month. Who knew that you could make this sort of money legally?'

Several months later, Annette, Errol, and Squirrel are returning to the club after a night out. As they approach the club, an air-car glides past them and pulls up outside the club. It is long, black with gold trim, and a golden dragon on the bonnet. Two doors open, and two figures get out, dressed in black and clearly armed. They scan the crowd. Squirrel gasps. 'That air-car is a Holden Royale. With the triple expansion star drive, there were only three ever built. They are worth squillions.' As they approach the car, one of the guards opens a rear door. A man alights, just over five feet tall, with oriental features and a yellow complexion. He is wearing a gold robe. He addresses the trio. 'Ah, I see that you like my Dragon. Yes, she is indeed beautiful and so fast with every comfort. Allow me to introduce myself. I am One Hung Low. If I had any friends, they would call me One. You will call me Mister Low. Let us adjourn to your fine establishment; we have business to discuss.' They are sitting in a booth at the rear of the club, it is late, with only a few customers left. The staff are starting to clean up.

Mr Low summons one of the guards. 'Allow me to order: a golden tonsil tickler for you, Errol; a beer for Annette; and a white wine for Squirrel. Mongrel, if you would.' The guard goes to the bar and returns with the drinks. Errol stares at Mr Low. 'So what the hell is this all about? I don't think that we have any business to discuss with you.' 'That is where you are wrong, my dear Errol. Tomorrow, one of my accountants, a Mr Chong, will come and go over your books. Then, on the first of every month, Mongrel here will come and collect ten percent off the takings, a tax if you will.' Annette rises. 'I don't bloody think so. You can take your ten percent and your Mr Chong and shove them up your arse.' Mr Low shakes his head. 'Oh dear, you don't think that I am serious. Mongrel, if you will.' Mongrel draws a laser and starts shooting bottles behind the bar. The bar staff duck below the bar, screaming, while Mongrel, laughing, starts on the ceiling lights. Errol stands and shouts. 'Alright, alright, that will do. Send your Mr

Chong.' Mr Low stands, gives a small bow. 'I am so glad that commonsense has prevailed. I will bid you good night.' They have cleaned up the mess and sent the staff home with a bonus. Now they are in the office. Annette is furious. 'I'm not going to give that bastard one credit.' Squirrel agrees. 'We have fourteen days before the end of the month.' One of my grifter friends once told me, 'If you want to get at someone, take what they love most.' 'I suggest a pre-emptive strike.' Annette agrees. 'How about we get Pluto to do some research on Mr Low. We have fourteen days before the end of the month.' Three days later, they meet for a council of war. Pluto begins. 'Mr One Hung Low is not to be taken lightly. He is one of the city's most successful and notorious gangsters. The only thing that he seems to care about is his air-car, his Golden Dragon. If you attack him in any way, you will have to leave this planet, or he would track you down. From what I have been able to gather, your deaths would be slow and painful.' 'If we could steal his Golden Dragon, I think that I have just the person who would gladly buy it for cash,' says Errol. 'Arthur Corkscrew is a friend of mine. He is a purveyor of pre-loved starships, spaceships, and air-cars. I have helped him out in the past. I have a small starship stored in a hangar here that has room to fit the Golden Dragon. I will call him and see how much he is willing to pay us for it.' Errol goes to his ship and fires up his Starlink, tapping in a series of numbers. A hologram appears. It shows a large man with a green complexion. He is wearing a bright red suit with a yellow shirt. 'Errol, my boy, it has been too long. How are you?' 'I'm fine, thank you, Arthur. I have a question. If I had a Holden Royale air-car that I wanted to sell, would you be interested?' 'My son, I have never seen one, but of course I know of them. The finest air-car ever built. If you did have one, it would be, as we say in the trade, to have fallen off the back of a truck. But we also say, never look a gift horse in the mouth. If you had one, what sort of price would you be looking at?' 'For you, Arthur, a mere one hundred and fifty thousand credits.' 'My son, you have yourself a deal, cash on delivery.'

It's three am. The club is deserted and dark. Errol is dressed in dark camo, taking things from a backpack and placing them around the club. Squirrel enters through the rear door, also dressed in dark camo. 'I've paid off the staff and told them that the club is closing. Pluto and I boosted an air-car; it's parked out the back. How are you doing?' 'Great. I'm just setting some little surprises for whoever tries to get in.' Annette enters, dressed in space armour, with a magnum forty-seven on each hip. She hands Errol a long-range laser.

Squirrel exclaims, 'Whoa! Look at you two!' Annette replies, 'Yeah, well, we weren't always barkeepers. So, to run through the plan again. When we get to One Hung Low's villa, Pluto will get us past the security into the villa. The Royale is kept in a glass-plastic box in front of the villa. Pluto will get the doors open. Once inside, Errol and I will keep the guards off until you and Pluto get past the Royale's security systems. Then we're away.' They arrive at the villa in the early hours of the morning. Squirrel takes out Pluto. Pluto says, 'I have disabled the alarm on this side door; I will now open it. There we go. I will now turn off the scanners in the grounds.' They move through the grounds and arrive at the box where the Royale is kept. Pluto scans and opens the doors. Pluto continues, 'Now we come to the tricky bit,' 'The Royale's security system will only respond to its owner. But if the maintenance computer tells it that a service technician needs to enter and do a test flight, it will allow us to enter and fly it. It will take me about five minutes to do this.' They are in the box when suddenly the grounds are flooded with light. A voice booms out. 'Ah, the scum from the club. If you do any damage to my Dragon, you will have a painful death. Surrender now and I may spare you.' 'Errol yells to Annette, Here come the guards. They will have their lasers on stun so as not to damage the Royale. We don't have that worry. Let's take 'em down.' Laser's flash through the night. Pluto's voice echoes, 'We're in. I'll open the driver's side door.' Errol dives in and gets behind the controls. The voice of One Hung echoes across the grounds. 'Fools! You won't be able to go anywhere. The controls will only respond to me.' Pluto fires up the car; they reverse out and power across the grounds. One Hung shouts, 'WHAT! That can't happen. Stop! My dragon! I will track you down and make you pay.'

They fly to the hangar where Errol keeps his ship and park the Royale inside. Errol takes the controls. They are ecstatic. Errol says to Annette, 'Just like the old days, Annie.' And they fly off.

THE END

Retribution

The door of the truck opens, a man steps onto the two steps then down onto the road. He is dressed in a hi-vis shirt with the sleeves cut off at the shoulders, black shorts, and sand shoes. He is rather tall with grey hair and a paunch. He looks up and down the highway. Nothing, except stunted bushes and silence. He stretches and walks around to the offside of the truck. Looks out across the landscape, the sun is just coming up. He pisses onto the sand with a sigh of relief. Once done, he opens a toolbox and retrieves a long-handled hammer. He walks along the length of the truck. It is an Australian road train with three trailers. He walks down the length of the train, banging each tyre with the hammer, looking for deflating tyres. He completes his check and not finding any problems, returns the hammer to the toolbox. He hears a vehicle and looks up. A pale green older model Toyota Land Cruiser camper pulls up behind his rig.

    The driver's door opens and out steps a woman. She is petite, maybe one hundred and forty centimetres tall, with short blonde hair and a figure that a lot of woman would kill for. She is wearing a white blouse, a short dark skirt, with ankle boots. She goes to the front of the Cruiser, lifts the bonnet, and leans into the engine bay, revealing a lot of stocking-clad leg.

'Must be my lucky day,' he thinks as he approaches her. 'Need any help?' he asks.

She turns to face him, her voice husky with a trace of an accent. 'My alternator light has come on and the temperature gauge has gone into the red.'

He gives her his best smile. 'Let's have a look-see.' He looks into the engine bay. 'Yeah, as I thought, you've lost your fan belt,' he says. He faces her and looks at her legs. 'You had better take off those pantyhose.'

She backs up, with her hands in the air. 'Please don't hurt me, I have money.'

He smiles. 'No, love, you've got it all wrong. See, with a pair of pantyhose, I can probably make a temporary fan belt that will get you to the next roadhouse, about fifty k's away.'

She drops her hands, embarrassed. 'I'm sorry, I've got a spare pair in the back, I'll get them and the toolbox.'

She goes to the back of the cruiser and returns with a packet and a small toolbox. 'Here you are.' 'Okey-dokey, let's see what we can do.' He takes a couple of spanners from the box and leans into the engine bay. He senses her behind him and goes to look at her when he feels a blow to the back of his head. He sees stars and then blackness. He slumps off the car and falls onto his back onto the gravel. She stands over him holding a club in both hands. He moans and she brings the club down onto his head.

She looks up and down the highway. Nothing. She goes to the back of the car and returns with a fan belt that she had removed previously. She quickly reattaches it, tensions it, and closes the bonnet. She gets in the car, does a U-turn, and backs the cruiser up to the man. When she gets out, she has a length of rope. She ties one end around the man's ankles, the other end she ties to the tow bar. After one more check of the highway, she gets in the car, starts it, and takes off, turning onto a track that heads into the bush and accelerates. The vehicle, towing the good Samaritan, disappears in a cloud of dust.

Sometime later, a road train pulls into the truck bay. It has the same livery paintwork as the one that is already parked there. It pulls up alongside. The engine shuts down, and a man steps down from the cab and goes over to the other truck. He steps up to the cab and bangs on the window. 'What are you doin', ya lazy bastard? 'You should be unloading in Alice!' There is no answer. He tries the door handle, and to his surprise, it opens. 'Hey, Fred, you there?' No answer. He climbs into the cab and looks in the sleeper cab; it's empty. Then he notices that the keys are in the ignition. 'Whoa, what's going on here?' He steps down from the cab and walks around the truck, calling Fred's name. No answer. He returns to his truck, climbs in, and hits a number on the phone.

A woman answers, 'Acme Freight Company, how can I help?'

'G'day, Pam, Bob here. Can I speak to the boss?' 'Sure, Bob, I'll put you through.' Before Bob can speak, a gruff voice comes on the line. 'Bob, where the hell is Fred? I've had the warehouse in Alice on my back wanting to know where their load is.'

'Well, boss, I'm looking at their load right now. The only trouble is, no Fred.'

'What? Where the hell are you?' Bob explains about the truck and the missing driver.

'Jesus, this is going to turn into a clusterfuck. I'll call the cops and get back to you.'

Ten minutes later, the phone rings. 'Yeah, boss,' he answers. 'They are going to send out the Sargent from Coopers Crossing. They reckon he should be there in under an hour. In the meantime I'll see about sending a driver out to get that load to Alice. While you're waiting, have a look around.' 'Okay, boss, will do. See ya.' Bob is laying in his bunk when he hears the sound of a siren fast approaching. A police cruiser roars into the truck bay and pulls up alongside the trucks. The engine and siren stop, but the lights keep flashing. Bob climbs down and goes to meet the officer. 'G'day, I'm Bob Stevens.' The officer shakes his hand. 'Seargent Nick Garfront. So, what's the story?' Bob tells him what he knows.

'Alright, I'll have a look around and check out the cab, then get on the blower and see if I can get a mustering chopper from a station to have a look. If we don't find him, I'll notify C.I.D in town.'

It's just after 11 pm, and the bar at the Wombat Springs Hotel has closed. A man heads towards the parking bay at the rear of the hotel. He is unsteady on his feet, suggesting that he has been propping up the bar for a while. He walks through the gloom. As he gets towards the far side of the truck bay, he approaches a Land Cruiser parked at the edge of the bush. There is a woman sitting at a table. On the table is a lamp that puts out a low light, a bottle, and two glasses. He eyes the woman; she is attractive with long dark hair. She is wearing a tee shirt and obviously no bra, with a short skirt. He changes direction and approaches her. 'Nice night for it,' he says.

'It sure is,' she replies. 'Care for a nightcap?' 'I could use the company.' 'That would be my pleasure,' he replies. 'Have a seat. I've got bourbon with Coke, soda, or water.' He sinks into the chair. 'Bourbon with Coke would be great.' She pours him a drink and holds out her hand. 'Ann's the name.' He takes her hand. 'Well, I'm very pleased to meet you. I'm Luke. I must say, Ann, you're a very attractive woman. What brings you out to these parts?'

'Oh, just got sick of the city, all the pretentious crap. Thought that it was time to go bush and meet some real people. What about you?'

'That's my rig over there,' he points to a road train about fifty metres away. 'I'm an owner-operator. Got to operate too.' They've had several drinks. She leans over and kisses him; they become passionate. She whispers in his ear, 'I've never made love in a truck before.' He takes her by the hand. 'Well, this is your lucky night.'

'As well as mine,' he thinks.

They go hand in hand to his truck. He unlocks the cab door. She kisses him and says in that husky voice, 'I'll get in, then you get in the sleeper and lay down, and I'll do what I do best.' He eagerly agrees. After she enters, he climbs in the sleeper cab, closes the door, and lays down on his back. She leans over him from the front seat. In the dim light, he sees a flash of silver. She thumps him in the chest. The pain. Twice more her hand rises and falls. The pain fades to blackness.

She wipes the stiletto on his shirt, takes the keys from his pocket, climbs down from the cab, and looks around. All is quiet. She locks the cab, pockets the keys, and returns to the cruiser.

It is first light, the sun not up yet. A light green Land Cruiser pauses at the edge of the highway. Left is North. Right is South. It hesitates a moment, then the left blinker comes on. The cruiser disappears into the early morning mist.

The phone rings in the office of the Wombat Springs Hotel. 'Wombat Springs Hotel, Brian speaking,' 'Hi, my name is Sue Wellspring. My partner is a truckie. He calls me every night to let me know that everything is alright. If we don't connect, he leaves a message. Last night he didn't call. I have tried to call him, but it just goes to voicemail. The last time he called was from your hotel on Tuesday night. He said that he was going to have a feed, get some sleep, and be on the road before daylight. It's now Thursday. He has never gone this long without contacting me.'

'What's his name and what is he driving?' 'His name is Luke Springload. Our truck is a Kenworth, pulling a b-double. It's green with S and N freight signage.'

'It might be parked out the back. Give me your number, and I'll go and have a look and call you back.' 'Thank you, I would be most grateful.'

'Hello, it's Brian from Wombat Springs.' 'Yes, Brian, what can you tell me?' 'Your rig is definitely here, it's locked. I've asked the staff, and he was here and had a meal in the bar. I don't think that anyone has seen him since. We do have a police station in town if you would like to call them, I can give you their direct number.' 'That would be great, thanks.'

'Senior Constable Bonnet of Wombat Springs receives a phone call from a Sue Wellspring concerning her partner. He takes the details and tells her that he will check it out and get back to her. He drives to the hotel. Sure enough, the truck in question is there. He knocks and tries the doors. They are locked, and he can't see into the sleeper because a curtain is drawn.' Next, he questions the Manager and the staff. The last person to have seen him was the barmaid when she closed the bar. 'Okay,' he decides, 'we need to get into the cab.'

He drives to the truck and machinery workshop, gets out, and walks into the service bay. A man in overalls is filling in paperwork at a bench. The constable approaches him. 'G'day, Mike, how's it going?' 'Fine, thanks, Bill, what can I do for you?'

'Would you be able to pop the door locks on a Kenworth prime-mover?' 'Sure, no probs, what's the deal?'

'Can you come down to the truck bay at the back of the pub? I'll explain when we get there.' 'Sure, I'll be about fifteen minutes, see you there.'

They meet at the truck bay, Mike takes a tool from his box, climbs up to the passenger side door, inserts the tool into the lock, gives it a jiggle and unlocks the door. He steps down, 'There you go, Bill.' The Constable steps up, opens the door, moves inside, and draws back the curtain. 'JESUS. Houston, we have a problem.'

It's early evening in an abandoned road quarry. A pale green Land Cruiser camper is parked. A woman is sitting underneath an awning. In front of her, a small fire emits a rosy glow. Alongside her is a table, on which is a wine bottle in an ice bucket. She leans back and sighs, enjoying the quiet.

She sees the headlights first and then hears the vehicle. It is coming along the same track that she used. She sighs, stands up, and goes to the back of the Cruiser, takes something out of the back, and returns to her chair. She is taking a sip of wine when the car bursts into the quarry with a roar. It slides to a halt in front of her. Loud music pumps from the car. The engine and the music stop. The driver's side and the passenger side doors open, and two men get out. They are both wearing blue singlets and shorts, both have straggly hair and beards, and tattoos. They lean against the car, looking at her. Both have bottles in their hands. The bigger one speaks. 'Well, bro, look what we got here. A lady that would like to have a drink and some fun with us.' The shorter one has a drink, burps, and says, 'Lady, it's your lucky night.' She looks at them and says in a husky voice, 'I'm giving you one chance to go away.' The big one laughs. 'Oh yeah, is little you going to make us go?'

'No, not me. Mr Colt,' she raises the handgun in a two-handed grip, aims at the big man. BOOM, BOOM. He slams back against the car and falls to the ground. She turns to the other man, his mouth opens, and he drops the bottle. BOOM, BOOM. He falls to the ground. After the noise, the silence is deafening. She puts the gun on the table and raises her glass, drinks.

After a few minutes, she puts on a small headlamp, packs up, rolls up the annex, and douses the fire. From the back of the cruiser, she takes a jerry can, undoes the cap, fits on the funnel, and being careful not to get any on herself, she dowsers the two bodies and then pours some into the car. She replaces the jerry can and starts the cruiser. As she drives past, she flicks out a burning box of matches.

As she drives out of the quarry, the car goes up with a roar.

A pale green Land Cruiser comes out of a bush track and faces the highway. Left is East, right is West. It hesitates as if perhaps someone is tossing a coin. After a moment, the left indicator flashes, the car turns, and the tail lights disappear into the night.

THE END